Adventures of the Arabian Nights

An imprint of Om Books International

Reprinted in 2018

An imprint of Om Books International

Corporate & Editorial Office
A 12, Sector 64, Noida 201 301
Uttar Pradesh, India
Phone: +91 120 477 4100
Email: editorial@ombooks.com
Website: www.ombooksinternational.com

Sales Office
107, Ansari Road, Darya Ganj,
New Delhi 110 002, India
Phone: +91 11 4000 9000
Fax: +91 11 2327 8091
Email: sales@ombooks.com
Website: www.ombooks.com

ISBN: 978-81-87107-95-8

Printed in India

10 9 8 7 6 5 4

Contents

Sindbad and the Porter

A long time ago in Baghdad, lived Hindbad, a poor porter who used to carry heavy loads every day.

One day, while carrying a heavy load, he sat down to rest in front of a palace. The grandeur of the palace made him

curious of how rich the people living inside would be. When he asked a passer-by about who lived in the palace, he was told that it was the house of Sindbad — the famous sailor — who had travelled to many distant lands.

Hearing about Sindbad, Hindbad looked at the sky and shouted loudly, "God! I, Hindbad, am a poor porter and have to carry such heavy loads for every single meal and right here, lives Sindbad, in so much pomp and wealth.

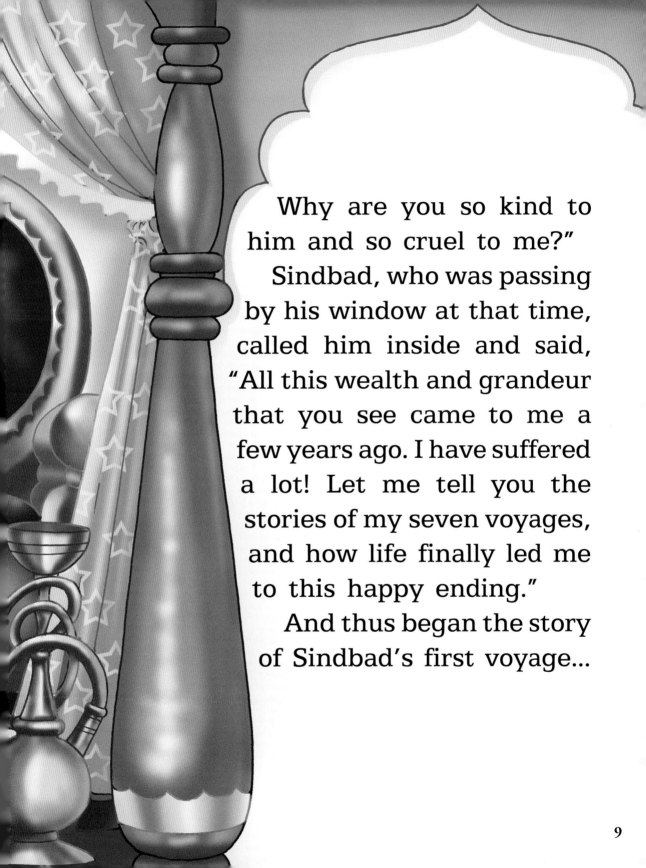

Why are you so kind to him and so cruel to me?"

Sindbad, who was passing by his window at that time, called him inside and said, "All this wealth and grandeur that you see came to me a few years ago. I have suffered a lot! Let me tell you the stories of my seven voyages, and how life finally led me to this happy ending."

And thus began the story of Sindbad's first voyage...

First Voyage

Sindbad began his story at the feast he had for Hindbad. "I was born to rich parents and gambled away all the money. One day, I realized that I was not living life the right way and became a trader."

"I set sail to distant lands on a ship. One day, our ship stopped at a place on the seas, where there was an island. The captain

asked us to relax on the island. My friends and me lit a small fire and were about to start eating, when suddenly we felt the island trembling. The place we thought was an island was actually the back of a sleeping whale! So, the whale suddenly moved and

dived into the depth of the ocean. My friends who were near the ship got into it, but I was left only with a piece of wood that I had used to light the fire. Holding on to that wood, I kept afloat all night and day," said Sindbad.

"The next day, I found a small patch of land and found some fruits to eat. While eating, I saw a horse tied to a tree. I went close to it and could hear some voices coming

from under the ground. I then saw men coming out of a cave. They were the servants of King Mihrage," continued Sindbad.

"They took me to their King, who welcomed me with open arms and ordered his servants to take care of me. As luck would have it, while sitting on the shore one evening, I saw a ship anchoring. The Captain of the ship was getting his men to move some huge boxes on to the shore. I could see my name written on the boxes. I recognized the Captain and ran to him. But he did not believe I was

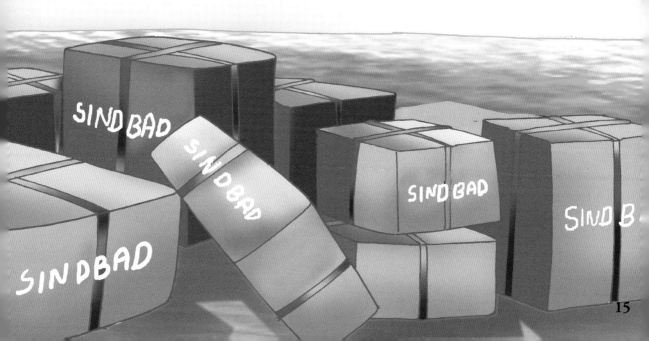

Sindbad. I had to tell him the story of the whale and my meeting King Mihrage to make him believe that I was truly the Sindbad he knew."

"I got my boxes back from the Captain. I gave a gift to King Mihrage and left for Balsora. I earned a hundred thousand sequins on my way back and was received with great happiness by my family," said Sindbad.

Sinbad then told Hindbad, "Take these hundred coins and enjoy tonight with your family. But come back tomorrow to hear about my next voyage."

Second Voyage

"My second voyage saw me facing more frightening adventures," said Sindbad to Hindbad, who had come back the next day.

"A few years after my first voyage, I set out again to distant lands. The ship that I had set sail on had anchored at a place. My

friends went in search of food, while I rested and fell asleep under a tree. When I awoke, the ship had gone, leaving me on that island!"

"I climbed up a tree to find out where I was and saw a dazzling white object quite far away. When I drew closer, I saw the light came from a round white object, which was huge in size. I suddenly saw a huge black cloud coming near me. When the cloud came near, I saw that it was in fact a bird and the white object was the bird's egg!"

"I had heard travellers talk about a bird called the roc, which was very large in size. The bird had come to keep its egg warm. When the bird settled on the egg, I removed my turban and tied myself carefully to one of its legs. After a few hours, when the roc took off, I had taken flight. I was not even one-tenth of its size!"

"I flew over the sea and many lands, till the roc decided to descend swiftly and kill a

snake. I quickly untied the turban and was again on land. But how I wish I had not done that! The island was the home of unbelievably large snakes. These snakes would come out only in the night, as the roc would kill them in daylight. Apart from the deadly snakes, the island also had large diamonds," said Sindbad with a smile. "So I lived in a small cave and shut it with big stones during the night and would come out

only in the mornings. One day, I was sitting on a rock, when I saw a big chunk of meat lying next to me. I saw that such chunks were lying at quite a few places. I remembered tales of merchants who would throw meat pieces into the valley of diamonds, when the eagles had their young. The eagles would pick up the meat to carry back to their newborn, and the meat would have a few pieces of diamonds stuck to it. The merchants would

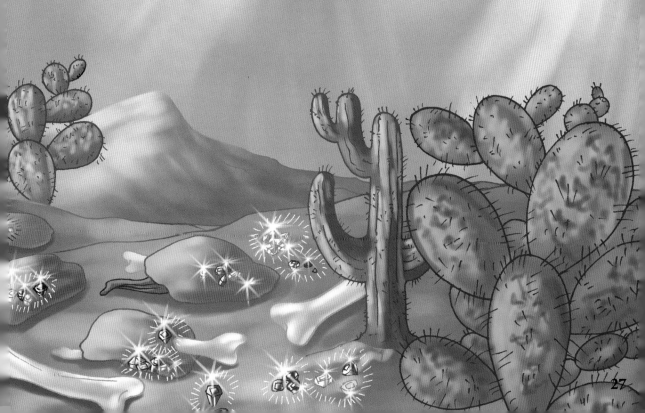

collect their pieces by shooing away the birds after they fed their young."

"So, that is what I did my friend. I waited for a big eagle to descend for the meat and held on to its leg. I flew with it to its nest

and cried out for help when the merchants came near! I shared my diamonds with the merchants and brought plenty of them home after my second voyage!"

Third Voyage

"In my third voyage, I had set off from Balsora. My ship faced a terrible storm and the Captain anchored the ship near an island. He told us that scary dwarves lived on this island. No sooner had he said this, we saw a huge number of small dwarves with red fur on their bodies swimming in the waves and coming towards our ship. They got on to our ship and drove it to another strange island. They left us on the shore and took away the ship," said Sindbad.

"We walked around for hours and finally found a palace. When we entered it, we found a huge pile of human bones! Before we could run outside, the huge door was flung open by a horrible-looking giant. He was as tall as

a palm tree, with just one eye. He stormed inside and picked me up. I was as small as a cherry in his hand. After checking how thin I was, he put me down and chose the Captain of our ship for his meal that day."

"The giant continued killing one person everyday. Finally, one morning, I struck upon a plan with my friends to build small rafts with the wood that lay near the shore. At night, we would return to the palace, where one of my friends would get killed. One night,

after the giant had killed one of us, he went off to sleep. A few of us picked up the red hot iron on which he would roast people and plunged it into his eye. The giant got up screaming, but could not find us, as he was blinded. Then we fled from there on our rafts. Strangely, many more giants like the one we saw, rose from the waters and threw huge stones at us. Only my raft with two of my friends, escaped," said Sindbad.

"We reached another island in the morning, and while we were resting after eating fruits, we heard a loud hissing sound. Before we could understand what it was, we saw a large snake sliding towards us at great speed and

it gripped one of my friends. My friend and me fled to a tree and climbed it. But that night, the snake returned and took away my sleeping friend, who was just below me. I was so terrified that I ran to the sea to die there,

rather than at the hands of the snake. But luckily for me, I found a ship passing by. I waved my turban with all my might. When the ship came closer, I saw that it was the Captain from the ship of my second voyage.

He was carrying cargo in my name and when I told him my story, he recognized me and gave all my things back. I traded them on the way back to Baghdad and made lots of money," said Sindbad ending the story of his third voyage.

Fourth Voyage

"On my fourth voyage in the sea, my ship was again wrecked by a storm. A few of us were washed on to the shore of a strange island. We walked around for a few hours before finding some huts. We found tall, black men, who took a few of us to each of their

huts. There they gave us a few herbs to eat. I was careful not to touch it, as I did not see the black men eating it. But my friends eagerly ate the herbs and soon, became mad! Then the men gave them lots of rice and I understood that they were trying to make us fat before eating us. Since I never ate what they gave me, I became very thin. One day, while the black men were away, I escaped from my hut and ran to the forest," said Sindbad.

"After wandering for seven days, I found a few white men gathering pepper. I made friends with them and they took me to their country. I met their King who was very nice to me and gave me many gifts. I found that

everyone rode on horses without a saddle. So I made one with a craftsmen for the King. He was so happy with it that I was asked to make saddles for all the King's men. Then the King asked me to marry a lady and stay in their country, which I gladly did," said Sindbad.

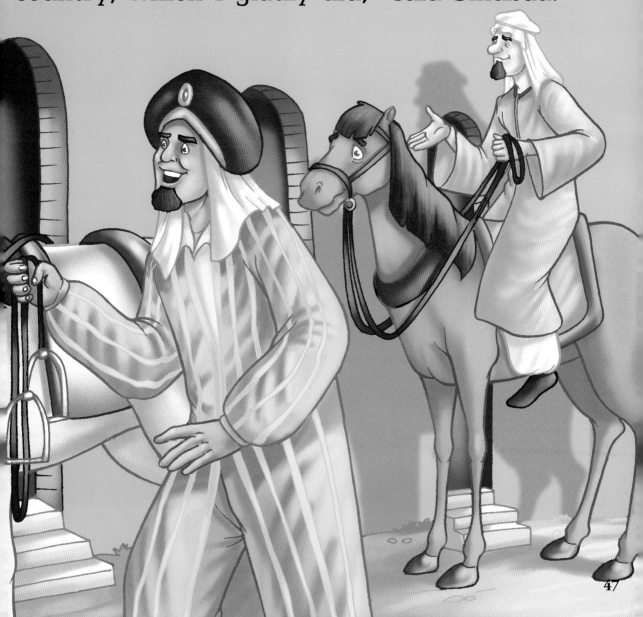

"One day, I heard a loud cry from my neighbour's house. I went to console him, but I learnt that it was the land's custom that if the wife or husband died, then their partner would also be buried alive along with them.

I was very scared hearing this. My fears were not wrong, as my wife took seriously ill and died after a few months. I was also lowered into a huge pit along with her body. I was given a few loaves of bread and some wine

to last me for a few days. I survived in the pit for a few days and just as I was to die of starvation, I saw the rock being moved and another woman with her dead husband being lowered into the pit. An idea struck me! I picked up a bone lying near by and hit the

woman on her head. Then I took her bread and wine and lived on it for a few days. I repeated this many times and thus, lived on for many days. Finally, I saw the shadow of a mouse running towards another end of the pit. I ran behind the shadow and came out of the pit on to the shores. Then I went back and collected all the gold and jewels that I could find in the pit and returned to the shore," said Sindbad with a smile!

"I was lucky to find a ship passing by, and I was brought home having collected enough wealth," said Sindbad ending his fourth voyage.

Fifth Voyage

"After sailing on other ships in my earlier voyages, I decided to build my own ship for my fifth voyage. I invited many merchants to join me and after sailing for a few days,

we anchored at an island. We found a roc's egg — the egg of the same huge bird, which I had seen before. Though I told the merchants not to touch it, they opened the shell and killed the little one," said Sindbad.

"When we set sail again, we saw the two huge rocs coming towards us. They were the parents of the little bird we had killed. They threw huge stones at us and our ship was broken into pieces. We were thrown into the sea, and I found myself washed on to an island. The island had lots of trees and lovely fruits. I ate those fruits and wandered around on the island till I saw a thin, old man sitting on a river bank. I thought he had also suffered a shipwreck. So I went and spoke to him. But he jumped on to my shoulders, wrapped his legs around my neck and started crushing it. I became dizzy and fell to the ground.

When I awoke, the old man kicked me towards the trees. He plucked fruits and ate all through the day. I had to suffer him on my shoulders for days."

"One day while passing through the island with the old man on my shoulders, I found my lost pitcher with some wine in it. I picked it up to have a sip. The effect was so strong that I did not feel his weight on my shoulders. The old man pulled it from me and also had a sip of it. Getting drunk, his hold on me

began to loosen and instantly, I pushed him off my shoulders and escaped from there. Once again, luck was with me and I found a ship passing by. When I got on to the ship and told them my story, the Captain told me that I had met the Old Man of the Sea, and it was my luck that he had not killed me like the others. On my way home, I traded in coconuts and pepper and came back home with lots of money as usual," said Sindbad.

Sixth Voyage

"On my sixth voyage, I sailed from a distant Indian port. But like all my other voyages, this time too, my ship was in deep trouble. Our Captain announced that we were caught in a wild current and there was no way to come out of it. The current pushed our ship near a mountain where no other ship or person would ever come."

"We looked all around us — there were rocks with precious gems studded — but there was no way out! Our Captain distributed the food we had between all of us and we were to live for the number of days the food would last. Meanwhile, I saw that there was a river with fresh water gushing out of the mountain, but not flowing into the sea."

"My friends did not last too long. Finally, after I had buried the last of my friends, I went to the river once more. I felt that the river had to be flowing out somewhere — if not the sea! So I decided to take a chance

and built a small boat and let myself flow out
with the river. My hunger made me dizzy on
the boat and I went into a deep sleep. When
I woke up, I saw men from another country
looking at me," said Sindbad with a smile.

"I was alive! I was taken to the King of that country, who heard my story and was delighted with it. After being the King's royal guest for a few days, I was put on a ship home with lots of costly presents to carry

back. The King gave me a precious vase for the Caliph of Baghdad. So my sixth voyage ended, with me a little more wealthy!" said Sindbad ending the story of his sixth voyage.

Seventh Voyage

"After all my voyages and the adventures I had faced, I decided to relax in Baghdad, but, I was visited by a messenger of the Caliph. He took me to meet the Caliph — the same Caliph for whom I had brought back a present in my last voyage," said Sindbad.

"Sindbad, I want you to take my gifts to the King," said the Caliph. "I tried my best

to avoid the voyage, but I could not. Finally, I sailed to the country I had visited on my sixth voyage and gave the presents to the King. On my way back to Baghdad, misfortune struck! My ship was seized by pirates and after taking all our belongings, they sold us as slaves," said Sindbad.

"I was the slave of a rich merchant. He took me to the forest with a bow and arrow to hunt elephants. He was a trader of elephant tusks. So, we would bury the elephant I would hunt and the merchant would get the tusks after a few days. This continued for a few weeks. One day, I was waiting in my hide-out trying to

spot an elephant. Suddenly, I saw a herd coming towards me. I was very scared as it seemed that they would crush me to death. But, the elephant, which came near me, picked me up with its tusk and put me on its back. Then, it took me into a dense forest, where we came to a large pit. It was as big as a

crater. There I saw the bones of all the dead elephants and a huge number of tusks," said Sindbad.

"It was the elephant's way of saying 'Take what you want and leave us!'. I went back to the merchant, who thought the elephants had killed me. I took him to the place where I

had spotted the tusks and from that day, the merchant was a very rich man. He freed me and put me on a ship back to Baghdad. Thus ended my final voyage with the teachings of an elephant and loads of money that the merchant had given me for showing him such a treasure," said Sindbad.

Hindbad went back home with his hundred coins for the day. More than the wealth he had earned in the last seven days, he had learned what it took to make such a wealthy and great man — lots of courage and determination!

OTHER TITLES IN THIS SERIES

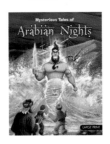

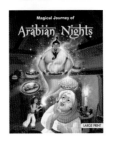